W9-CZW-755

Snap It!

Snapchat Projects for the Real World

Carolyn Bernhardt

Checkerboard Library

An Imprint of Abdo Publishing
abdopublishing.com

abdopublishing.com

Published by Abdo Publishing, a division of ABDO, PO Box 398166, Minneapolis, Minnesota 55439.

Printed in the United States of America, North Mankato, Minnesota

062016
092016

Content Developer: Nancy Tuminelly
Design and Production: Mighty Media, Inc.
Series Editor: Liz Salzmann
Photo Credits: AP Images; Mighty Media, Inc.; Shutterstock

Publishers Cataloging-in-Publication Data
Names: Bernhardt, Carolyn, author.
Title: Snap it! : Snapchat projects for the real world / by Carolyn Bernhardt.
Description: Minneapolis, MN : Abdo Publishing, [2017] | Series: Cool social media | Includes bibliographical references and index.
Identifiers: LCCN 2016936501 | ISBN 9781680783605 (lib. bdg.) | ISBN 9781680790283 (ebook)
Subjects: LCSH: Snapchat (Firm)--Juvenile literature. | Photography--Digital techniques -Juvenile literature. | Image processing--Digital techniques--Juvenile literature. | Internet industry--United States--Juvenile literature. | Online social networks--Juvenile literature. | Internet security measures--Juvenile literature.
Classification: DDC 775--dc23
LC record available at /http://lccn.loc.gov/2016936501

Contents

What Is **Snapchat?**

You're at a restaurant eating spaghetti. You remember that your cousin loves pasta. Your mom opens Snapchat on her smartphone and snaps a picture of you taking a bite. Your mom adds text to the snap. It says, "Enjoying your favorite meal!" Then she sends the snap to your cousin. Your cousin sees she has a Snapchat notification and opens the app. She laughs as she views the snap. After ten seconds, it disappears. This is the fun of Snapchat!

Snapchat is a photo- and video-sharing app. The messages users send are called snaps. Users edit snaps they create by adding **emoticons**, Geofilters, and face-changing effects. Users can also draw on their snaps, add **captions**, and apply **filters**. The possibilities are endless!

Snapchatters can send snaps directly to friends. Users can also make a string of snaps into a My Story for all of their friends to see. Once opened, snaps can only be viewed for up to ten seconds. Then, the images disappear. But a user's My Story can be watched over and over for up to 24 hours. Through Snapchat, users from around the world share original and fun moments with each other.

Snapchat
Site Bytes

Purpose: sharing photos and videos

Type of Service: app
App name: Snapchat

Date of Founding: July 13, 2011
(originally named Picaboo)

Founders: Evan Spiegel, Bobby Murphy, and Reginald "Reggie" Brown

Compatible Devices:

Tech Terms:

Geofilters

Geofilters are location badges that can be added to snaps. The badges feature drawings that relate to where the snap was taken. Snapchat uses **global positioning systems (GPS)** to detect a user's location. Then, that location's Geofilters become **available** to the user.

My Story

My Story allows users to combine a series of snaps to form a story. These stories can be viewed by all of their Snapchat friends.

Founding **Snapchat**

Evan Spiegel, Bobby Murphy, and Reginald "Reggie" Brown met at Stanford University in California. Brown noticed that people sometimes posted photos to social media that they later regretted. He wanted to create a way to send photos that disappeared after being viewed. Spiegel and Brown decided to make an app for sending disappearing photos.

Spiegel and Brown asked friend and computer scientist Bobby Murphy to help create the app. They named the app Picaboo. Picaboo was released in 2011. The app did not gain many followers at first. The company changed its name to Snapchat and continued working hard to promote it. Soon after, Snapchat took off. Today, Snapchat has more than 200 million users!

Evan Spiegel Bobby Murphy

Account Info:

- Users must be at least 13 to create an account.
- Snapchat can only be used on a smartphone or tablet.
- Once a user creates an account, he or she chooses a username.
- Users are given a Snapcode that can be scanned by other users to add them as friends. No two Snapcodes are the same.
- Users find friends by username, Snapcode, or phone number. Users become Snapchat friends once both users add each other.
- Only Snapchat friends can send each other snaps or view each other's My Story.
- Privacy **settings** allow Snapchatters to choose which friends can view their My Story.

Supplies

Here are some of the materials, tools, and devices you'll need to do the projects in this book.

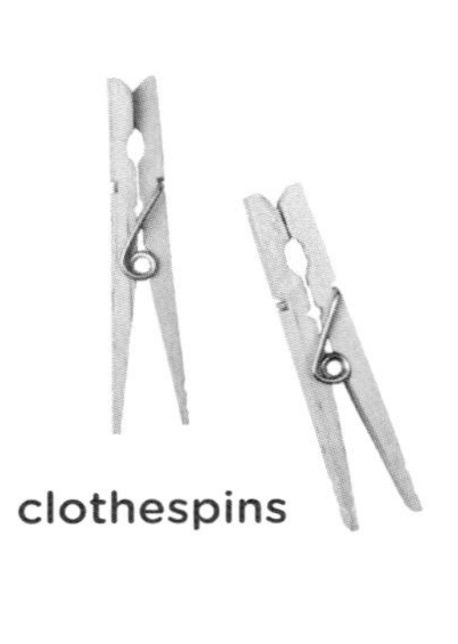

clothespins

photo frame

permanent markers

hole punch

cardboard

string

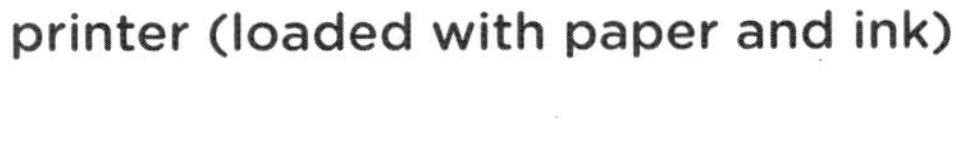

printer (loaded with paper and ink)

craft glue

craft knife

magnetic tape

scissors

tablet

smartphone

Staying Safe

The Internet is a great resource for information. And using it can be a lot of fun! But staying safe **online** is most important. Follow these tips to use social media safely.

* Never try to sign up for a social media account if you are underage. Snapchat users must be at least 13 years old.
* Don't share personal information online, especially information people can use to find you in real life. This includes your telephone number and home address.
* Be kind online! Remember that real people post content on the Internet. Do not post rude, hurtful, or mean comments. Report any instances of **cyberbullying** you see to a trusted adult.
* In addition to cyberbullying, report any **inappropriate** content to a trusted adult.

Safety Symbols

Some projects in this book require searching on the Internet. Others require the use of sharp or hot tools. That means these projects need some adult help. Determine if you'll need help on a project by looking for these safety symbols.

Hot!
This project requires use of a hot tool.

Internet Use
This project requires searching on the Internet.

Sharp!
This project requires use of sharp tools.

Real-Life Lenses

Take marvelous selfies with masks that mimic Snapchat Lenses!

What you need

- card stock
- pencil
- scissors
- cutting board
- craft knife
- various decorating materials, such as construction paper, craft foam, stickers, glitter, paint, crayons, colored pencils, markers, feathers, beads & buttons
- hot glue gun & glue sticks
- paint stir stick or large craft stick
- camera, tablet, smartphone

Snapchat Lenses are features that users can apply to photos. The lenses alter images of faces. Lens **technology** locates facial features. Then, the lens twists, enlarges, or otherwise changes certain features. The lens choices change often. One lens made the person seem to have huge eyes. Another added rainbows shooting from the person's mouth! Create your own **versions** of lenses to hold in front of your face and take funny photos.

1. Decide what type of lens you want to create. One that alters just one feature? Or a lens that covers your entire face?

2. Draw the shape of your lens on card stock. Draw where the eyes and mouth will be.

3. Cut out the lens.

4. Use a craft knife to cut out any eye, nose, or mouth holes. Ask an adult to help. Place the lens on a cutting board before cutting.

(continued on the next page)

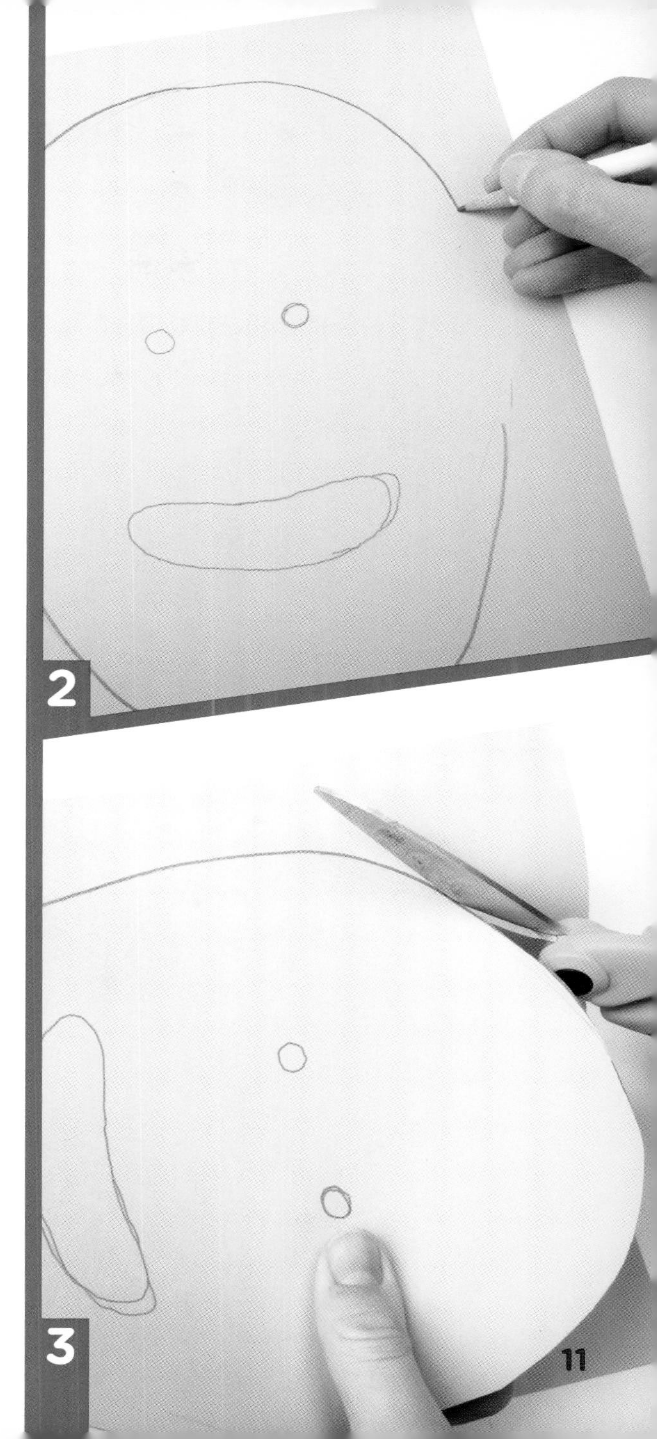

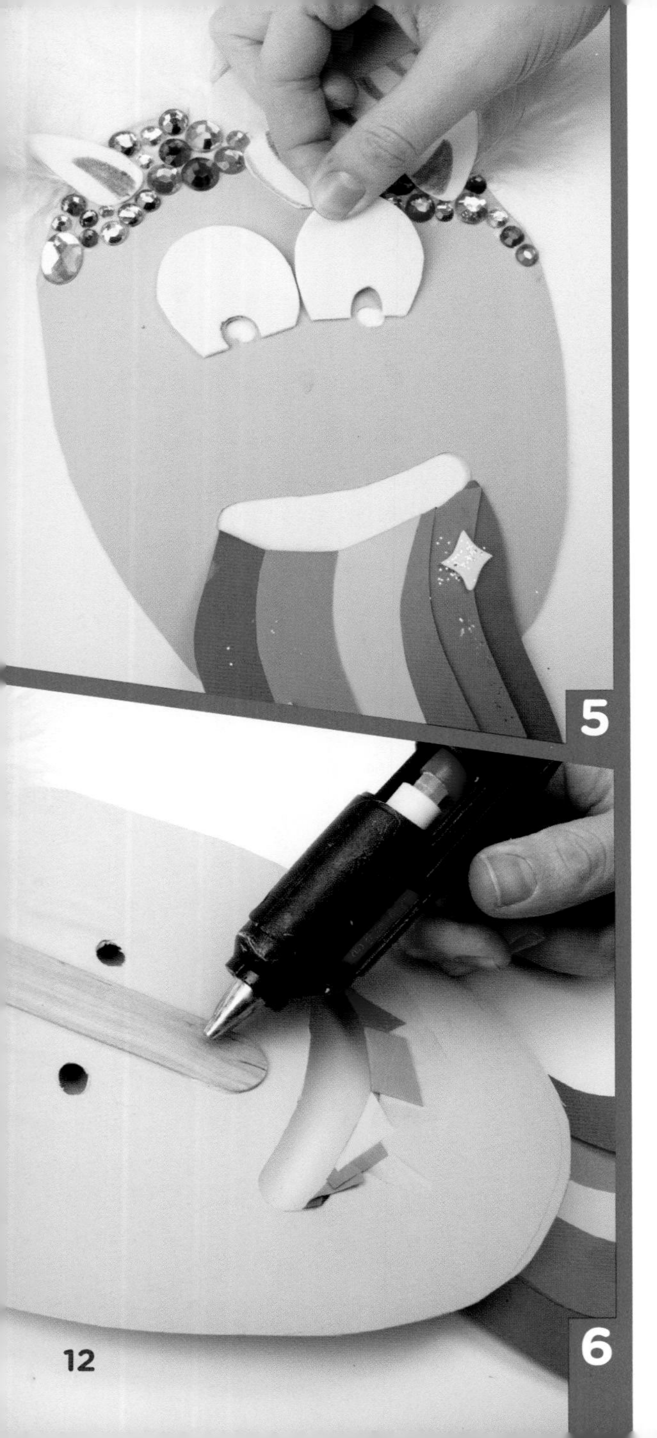

5. Decorate your lens however you like! Use construction paper to create rainbows, stars, or other shapes. Color with markers, colored pencils, crayons, or paint. Add stickers and glitter. Glue on beads, buttons, and more. Get creative!

6. Put hot glue on one end of the stir stick or craft stick.

7. Glue the stick to the back of the lens. The end without glue should stick out to use as a handle. Let the glue dry.

8. Hold the lens in front of your face. Have fun taking silly **selfies**!

Photo Painting

Add pizzazz to a printed picture using paint, stickers, and more!

What you need

- printed photo or a computer, printer & photo to print
- scissors
- cardboard
- markers, colored pencils, crayons, or paint
- round label stickers
- paper
- glue stick

Snapchat's editing tools allow users to draw on, color, and add fun stamps to their pictures. Recreate these fun features on a photo using art supplies.

1. Find a photo that you want to add fun features to. This could be a photo that is already printed. Or print a photo from your computer. It can be your own photo or one you find **online** with adult help.

2. Trim your photo to whatever shape or size you like.

3. Paint, draw, or color on the image.

4. Use markers to turn the label stickers into **emoticons**. Stick them to your photo.

5. Glue a strip of paper near the bottom of the photo. Write a **caption** on it.

6. Keep adding fun features until your photo looks just as you want it. Then, display it for everyone to admire!

#funfact

Every day there are 8 billion video views on Snapchat.

My Story Streamer

Tell a story through a string of pictures to hang in your room!

What you need

- printed photos or a computer, printer & photos to print
- scissors
- stickers
- markers
- paper
- craft glue
- string
- clothespins

My Story lets Snapchat users combine many photos to tell the story of their day. To do this, users **upload** snaps to My Story instead of sending them to specific friends. Photos in My Stories remain visible for 24 hours before disappearing. In this project, you will create a My Story from printed photos. But instead of disappearing, your string of photos can be viewed again and again!

1. Choose photos for your My Story. They could be from a vacation, a day of your life, or even your entire life! If the photos aren't printed, print them from your computer.
2. Trim the photos to roughly the same size.
3. Decorate the photos with stickers and markers. Glue on **captions** written on strips of paper.
4. Cut a long piece of string. Use the clothespins to hang your photos in **chronological** order on it.
5. Hang your My Story in your room!

Geofilter Frames

Create fun location-related filters to frame your photos!

What you need

- printed photo or a computer, printer & photo to print
- photo frame
- scissors
- clear cellophane
- permanent markers in assorted colors

A Geofilter is a badge on a Snapchat photo or video. The badge is a drawing that relates where the snap was taken. Geofilters are designed by Snapchat users. They create drawings for specific cities, states, and even countries. Then, users submit their drawings to the Snapchat team for review. Snapchat chooses its favorite images for a location and makes them into Geofilters. Then Snapchat uses **GPS** to make Geofilters **available** to users who are nearby. Users can then choose Geofilters for their snaps. In this project, you will create your own **versions** of Geofilters to frame photos from cool locations!

1. Select a fun photo of a location to frame. This could be a photo that is already printed. Or print a photo from your computer. It can be your own photo or one you find **online** with adult help.

2. Trim the photo to fit the frame.

3. Disassemble the frame. Use a permanent marker to carefully trace the glass on clear cellophane.

(continued on the next page)

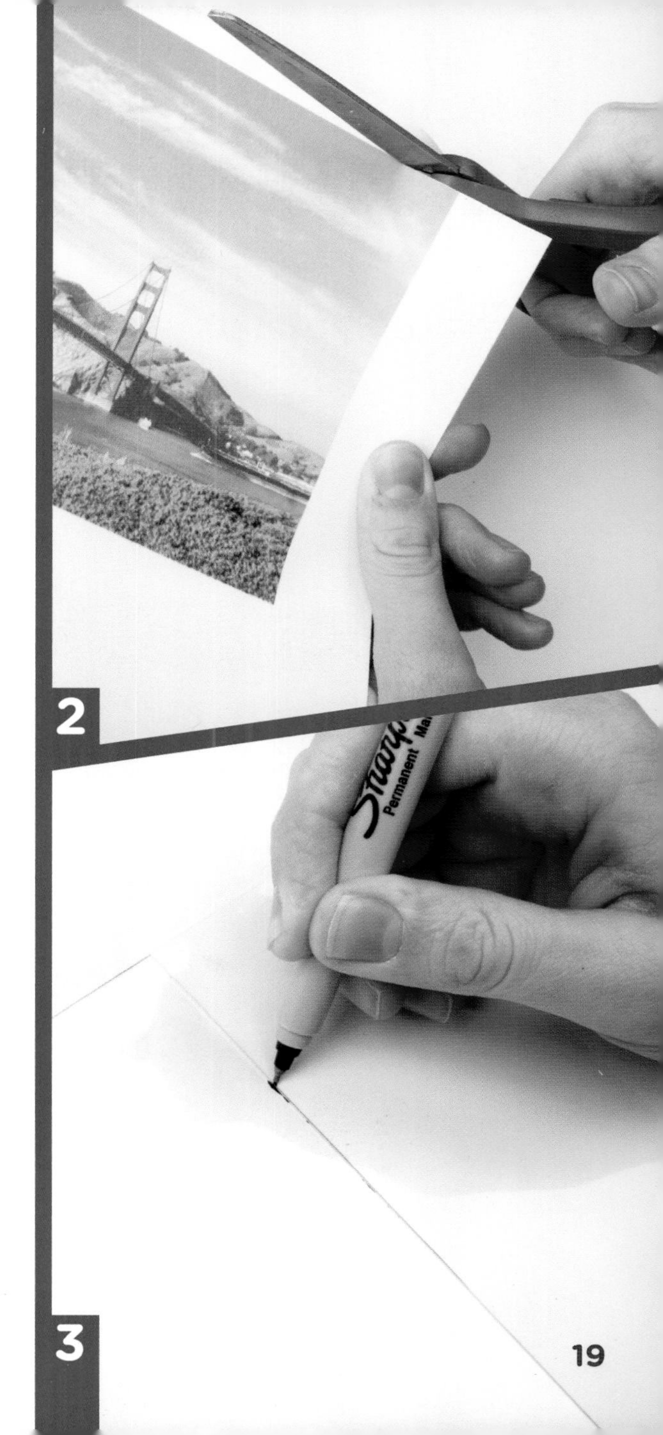

4. Lay the cellophane over the photo. Make sure the photo is inside the outline you traced.

5. Think of images, words, and colors that relate to the location in your photo. Draw your design on the cellophane. This is your Geofilter!

6. Cut out the Geofilter.

7. Reassemble the frame with the Geofilter between the photo and the glass.

8. Repeat steps 1 through 7 to create more location-related **filters**!

Mini Avatar Magnets

Create cool 3-D magnets resembling Snapchat's ghost logo!

What you need

» adhesive craft foam
» pencil
» scissors
» various decorating materials, such as stickers, glitter, markers & googly eyes
» craft glue
» nonadhesive craft foam
» magnetic tape

1. Draw a ghost outline on adhesive craft foam. Cut out the ghost.

2. Decorate your ghost however you like! Cut hats, clothes, or hair out of craft foam. Create a face with stickers or markers. Glue on googly eyes. Try making your ghost look like yourself or a friend or family member.

3. Cut a square background for your ghost out of nonadhesive craft foam.

#funfact

In 2015, 60 percent of high school seniors used Snapchat every day.

(continued on the next page)

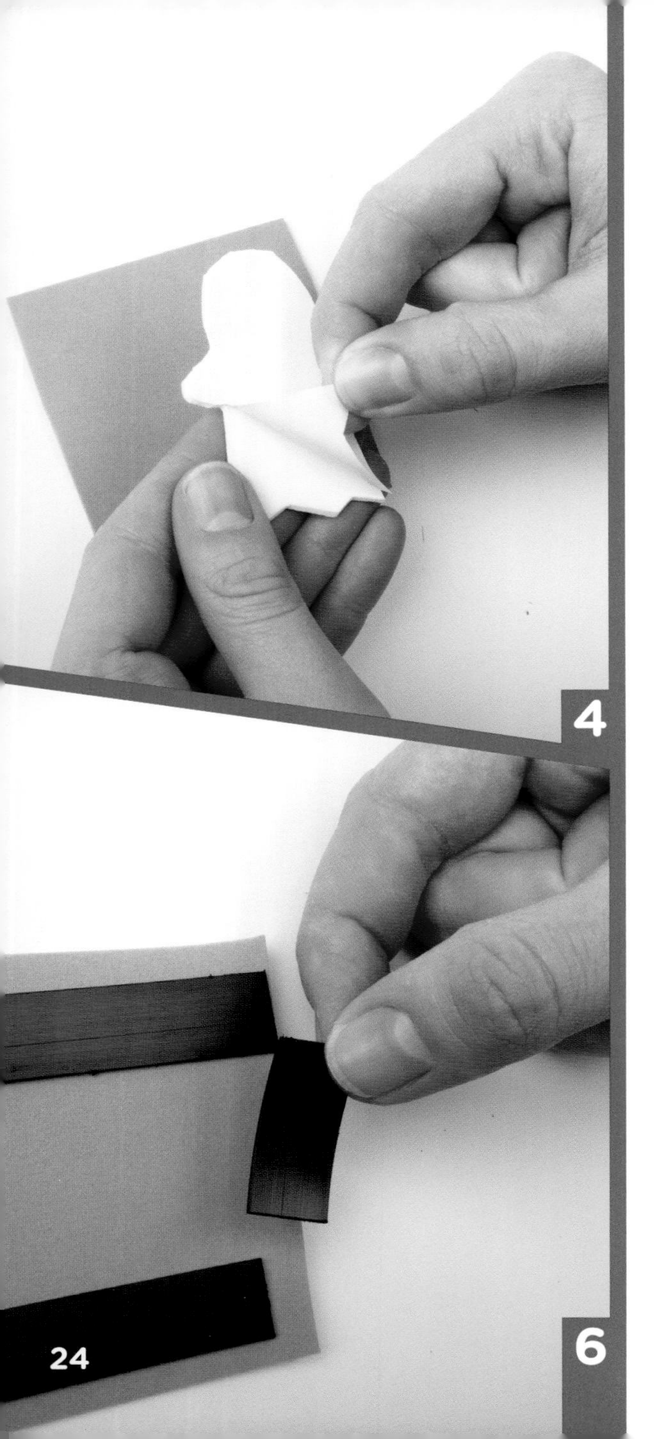

4. Peel the backing from the ghost and press it to the background.

5. Add decorations to the background if you want.

6. Cut short strips of magnetic tape. Stick the tape to the back of the craft foam.

7. Use your ghost magnet to hang a photo on your refrigerator or inside your locker at school. Or, give the ghost to a friend or family member!

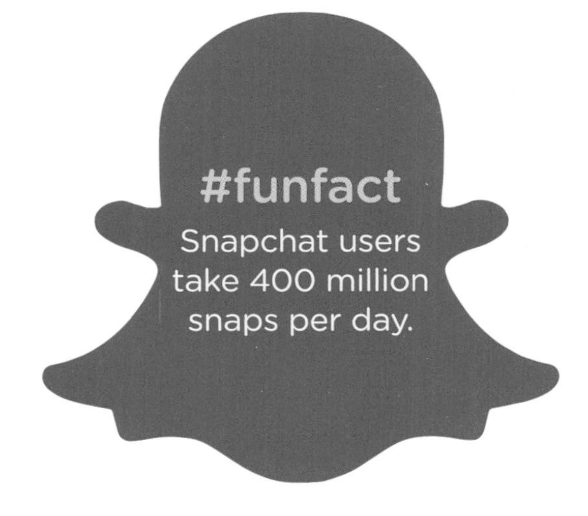

Group Gallery

Use photos from friends and family members to create a cool poster about an event!

What you need

- photos
- computer
- printer
- scissors
- markers
- poster board
- craft glue
- stickers or other decorations
- hole punch
- string

Snapchat has a fun, **collaborative** feature called Live Stories. This feature is a collection of photos and videos from Snapchatters at a certain location or event. **GPS** allows Snapchatters that are nearby to view the Live Story and submit photos or videos to it. The Snapchat team decides which snaps to add to the Live Story. In this project, you will create your own Live Story poster. It will include your photos from an event and photos sent to you from others who attended.

1. Choose an event to feature. It can be a family holiday or vacation, a school field trip, or a camping trip with friends. Find one or two photos that you took at the event. Print them out.

2. Ask others from the event for their photos. If needed, print the photos out. If any of the photos have a border, cut it off.

3. Choose a title for your gallery. Write the title across the top of the poster.

4. Arrange the photos you've gathered on the poster board. Glue them in place.

5. Decorate your poster! Draw designs with markers. Add fun stickers. Get creative!

6. When your gallery is complete, punch a hole near each top corner.

7. Cut a long piece of string. Tie one end through each hole.

8. Hang up your gallery and enjoy the **collaborative** memories of the event!

#funfact

71 percent of Snapchat users are younger than 25 years old.

Fast Forward and Rewind Flip-Book

Flip it forward or bend it backward!

What you need

- camera, smartphone, or tablet
- computer
- printer
- scissors
- optional: index cards, markers
- stapler

Snapchat allows users to do more than just send photos. Users can also shoot, edit, and send videos! Snapchat has editing tools that speed up or slow down video clips. Users can also choose to send their videos so that they play backward. You can create a physical **version** of a video that does the same thing! Turn action-packed photos into a fun flip-book. You can flip forward or backward as slowly or quickly as you like!

1. Find the burst function on your camera, smartphone, or tablet. Use it to take a series of photos of an action scene. This can be your sister's game-winning soccer goal or your cat jumping off the couch. Transfer the burst of images onto your computer and print them out. You should print at least four photos.

2. Trim your photos to the same size. Then skip ahead to step 4.

3. If you do not have a camera or computer, you can also draw a series of images. Think of an action scene. Draw the scene on an index card. Redraw the scene on more index cards, changing one thing each time to capture the action.

(continued on the next page)

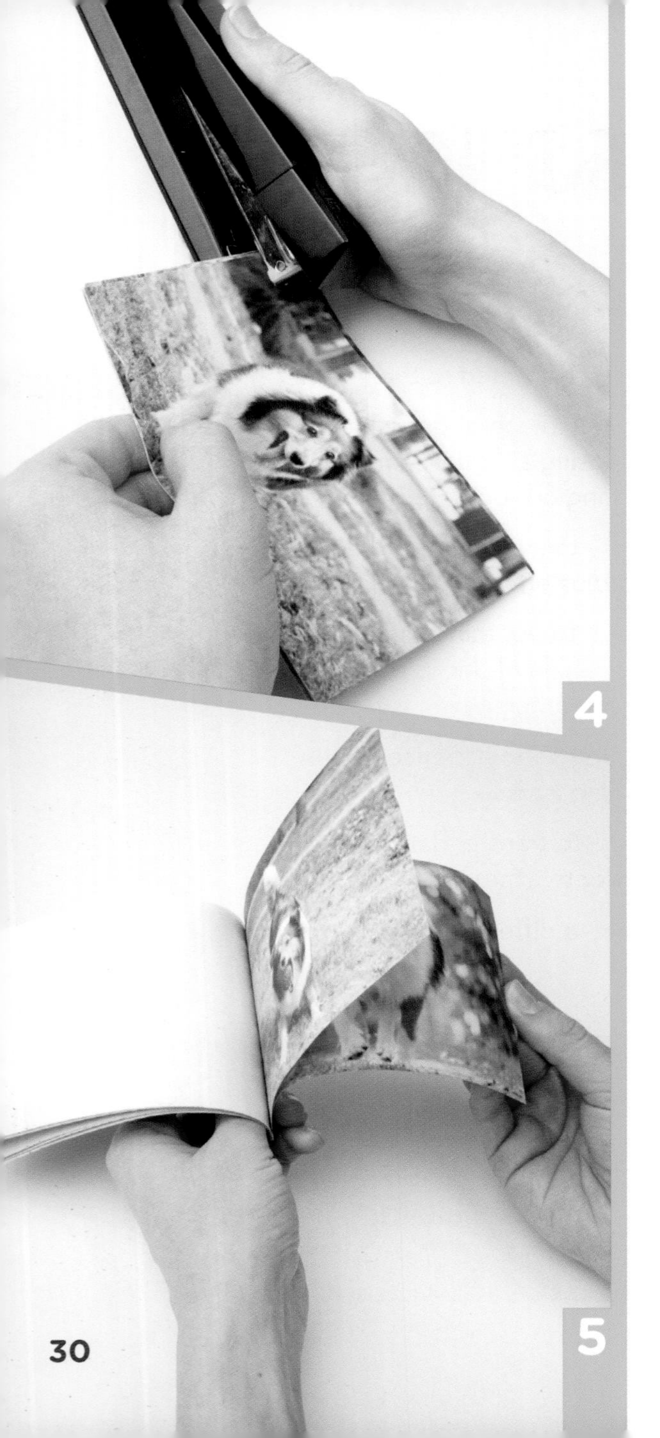

4. **Stack** the images in order. Staple the stack together along the left edge.

5. Flip through your book to watch the action unfold! Then flip through it the other way to watch it in reverse. Flip quickly, and then super slow. Do any of the flipping methods make the scene look silly? What other scenes might be fun to watch in reverse? Create more flip-books to find out!

#funfact

On average, Snapchat users spend 30 minutes a day using the app.

Glossary

available – able to be had or used.

caption – a written explanation of an image, such as a photo.

chronological – arranged in or according to the order of time.

collaborative – related to or resulting from working with others.

cyberbully – to tease, hurt, or threaten someone online.

emoticon – a small image used in e-mail and apps to communicate a feeling or attitude.

filter – a tool that can change the appearance of a photo.

global positioning system (GPS) – a space-based navigation system used to pinpoint locations on Earth.

inappropriate – not suitable, fitting, or proper.

online – connected to the Internet.

selfie – an image of oneself taken by oneself using a digital camera, especially for posting on social networks.

setting – the way a computer program is set or adjusted.

stack – 1. to put things on top of each other. 2. a pile of things placed one on top of the other.

technology – the science of how something works.

upload – to transfer data from a computer to a larger network.

version – a different form or type of an original.

Websites

To learn more about Cool Social Media, visit **booklinks.abdopublishing.com**. These links are routinely monitored and updated to provide the most current information available.

Index